SNO MONSTER

by

IAN BILLINGS

Find out more about Ian Billings at

www.ianbillings.com

@mrianbillings

GET YOUR FREE BOOK

VISIT HERE - http://eepurl.com/bt9RLP

Poems! Stories! Jokes! Limericks! And Cheese!*
Enter the kooky world of International Kid's Comic and Writer IAN BILLINGS as he rummages in his lost property box to bring you a bonkers book of stuff!
His silly style and wacky words will take you on a giggle-filled, chuckle-stuffed gallop through his mad mind!
There's chickens and fish and doors and octopuses and honey and tyres and noses and monsters and eggs and insects and pirates and holes and owls and geckos and clippings and mermaids and butter and spam and hiccups and cheese.**
If you like laughing, you'll like IAN BILLINGS' LOST PROPERTY!
* There's no cheese in it....
** There really isn't any cheese....

CHAPTER ONE

The black raven sat upon the bent and broken school gates as the rain slashed down. Its beady eye looked out across the school yard and it let out a cry.

On the gates was hung a cracked sign "St. Squirmings School for Ghouls and Monsters – Don't Wipe Your Feet!"

Through the gates was the school yard and on either side were grave stones. One read :

"Billy Twist. Very bad pupil. Maths 6/10, Geography 7/10. Will always be remembered for his sneezing."

Another read :

"Claire Grunt. One of our worst pupils ever. We are very proud of her. Never on

time. Would be late for her own funeral —
and she was."

Another :

"Jeremy Twitching — 1/10 English,
0/10 French, -1/10 Maths.
Once frightened a snail. A school legend."

The school gates creaked open to
allow a slow moving hearse through. It was
a long black slick car and the rain rattled
upon it.

The hearse drew up outside the school
gates and four pall-bearers slid the coffin
out of the rear. They placed it upon their
shoulders and walked slowly towards the
large wooden front doors of St.
Squirmings.

The dull bell sounded deep within the
building and the pall-bearers waited in the
cold, cold rain.

Eventually the doors creaked open
and a strange face emerged. It was the face
of an old man. A very old man. It was
Mr.Sneers, the Head Teacher.

"Can I help you?" he said in deep,
creepy voice.

"Yes!" said one of the pallbearers, "It's a delivery!"

Mr. Sneers opened the door further.

"I don't think we ordered anything..."

The pallbearers lowered the coffin onto the unwelcome mat and one produced a black clipboard.

"Just sign here, please!"

And Mr. Sneers signed and the pallbearers disappeared into the rain. The car screeched as it made off.

Mr. Sneers looked down at the coffin and sighed.

Then slowly, very slowly the coffin lid started to rise.

A smile slithered across Mr. Sneers' face.

Suddenly from out of the coffin leapt a small man with blond hair, dressed all in white and carrying a brief case.

He held out his hand.

"Hello, I'm Mr. Poke – the School Inspector!"

Mr.Sneers looked him up and down.

"Do come in!" he said, quietly.

And that was how St. Squirmings' Gruesome Inspection began. Word soon spread through the dark corridors of the school. Before long each pupil and each teacher knew about the inspection and all of them knew how important it was.

Mr. Poke peered into each room and tomb in the school. He looked into the Spot Squeezing Class (St. Squirmings had won many awards for this). He peered into the Food Technology Class (Mrs. Stain was teaching Mouldy Milk and Sour Cheese). He even dropped in on Mr. Clack's lecture on the History of Mud. In each class he made a mark in his book and moved on.

Eventually the inspection was complete and Mr. Poke handed his results to Mr. Sneers. St. Squirmings had come top of the Gruesome Inspections for the last five years. No one could better them. Mr. Sneers slid the report from the envelope.

He opened it.

He read it.

He looked up at Mr. Poke

Mr. Poke shrugged.

Mr. Sneers plucked a couple of hairs from his bushy eyebrows. Suddenly he exploded in rage.

"Bell, bell! Ring the bell, Mrs. Wart! Assembly, assembly!"

He screwed up the report and threw it after Mr. Poke, who was already scurrying for the door.

The entire school was soon gathered within the Great Ghastly Hall. The murmuring and mumbling disappeared as Mr. Sneers made his way onto the stage.

"As we all know the Gruesome Report is very important to us here at St. Squirmings. For the last five years we have been the highest achieving Ghoul School in the country."

He looked across at the faces of his pupils. He plucked another hair from his eyebrow. This was the sign of bad news and the pupils knew it.

"Until this year!" He slammed his hand on the podium and it wobbled slightly. "Because four pupils of this very school have let us down."

His eye fell on the second row.

"Somebody pick up my eye!"

Mrs. Grotter scuttled from behind the piano, picked up the glass eye and handed it back to him. He inserted it with a loud squelch. The assembly grinned proudly. That was the kind of grossness St. Squirmings was famous for, it was a pity they had been let down.

"Four pupils!" He scowled at the anxious faces and a little smoke came out of his ears.

Franny Stein and her monster, Gordon sat next to Wilf the Werewolf and he sat next to Benedict the headless monk. They all shuffled their feet embarrassingly and stared at the floor.

"You know who you are! St. Squirmings lost vital points for the following – Showing Consideration and Concern for Strangers..." Mr.Sneers paused whilst a mumble of disbelief tumbled through the room, "....making Happy Conversation during playtime." The mumble grew louder." And, finally, I'm so embarrassed one of my pupils did this - Helping a Little Old Lady Across the Road!"

His eyes scanned the whole school

"And I have the names! Franny Stein, Gordon, Wilf and Benedict!"

The assembly jeered.

"My office – ten minutes!"

Suddenly a small pellet hit Franny on the arm. She shrieked and held her shoulder.

"Who threw that?" demanded Mr.Sneers.

A dark figure stood up, silhouetted against the stained glass window. Mr. Sneers squeezed his eye and tried to see who it was.

There was a crack of thunder and a flash of light lit up the face of – Zack the Zombie.

The star pupil folded his arms and grinned proudly.

"Me, sir!"

"Very good, Zack!" said the Head. "But aim a little higher next time!"

Ten minutes later Wilf, Franny, Gordon and Benedict were standing outside the Head Teacher's office.

"What's wrong with helping a little old lady across the road when you want to?" asked Wilf. "If I want to be kind – I will!" He shook his long hair in disbelief at the situation.

Gordon twiddled with the bolts in his neck and spoke in a posh, educated voice, "Well, one has to admit the world would be a much happier place if we all showed each other a little kindness once in a while!"

Gordon was Franny's creation. She had made him from bits of old bodies and given him a human brain. She had wanted the brain of a criminal, so she could get him to go rampaging and things, but she had actually got hold of a professor's brain.

"Scratch my head, monster!" ordered Franny.

The monster sighed.

"I do wish you'd call me Gordon, mistress. Monster is such a common word!" he replied and scratched Franny's head.

Benedict the Headless Monk was tapping his foot with his arms folded. Suddenly, he stopped tapping. He made an "Ahh" sounded, but having no head it sounded a little odd. Then he did it a second time and then a third.

"Stand back!" yelled Wilf, "He's going to sneeze!"

And he did blow. A huge eruption of snot exploded out of his neck hole.

"Gross!" shouted Franny and Wilf, wiping themselves down. Gordon, being a well brought-up monster pretended it wasn't happening and stared out of the window.

Franny was wiping down Benedict's cowl when Mr.Sneers approached.

"What are you doing?"

"Cleaning up, Benedict, sir!" explained Franny.

"That's very *Kind* and *Considerate* of you!"

Wilf nudged her and she suddenly realised Mr.Sneers was being sarcastic.

"Yes, sir, sorry, sir!" She put away her hanky.

Mr. Sneers pointed to the office door.

"Inside now!" he ordered.

Wilf gestured to the door.

"After you, sir!"

Mr. Sneers stopped in his tracks and eyed Wilf with his one good eye.

"What did you say, boy?"

"After you, sir?" repeated Wilf, a little less confidently.

"Push in, boy, push in! Have you learned nothing here?"

So all five rushed the door and tried to elbow their way through. The door creaked open and they all fell through into the office.

It was a dark and dusty office. All over the floor were buckets and the rainwater plip-plopped into them. Papers and parchments covered the desk and on the windowsill (the window hadn't been washed for years) were some plants. As the five tumbled in the plants fluttered slightly and coiled up their leaves.

Mr. Sneers clambered to his feet and dusted himself down.

"Good effort."

He stalked over to his desk.

"Thank you, sir!" said Franny.

"Don't spoil it by being grateful!"

He grabbed a remote control, switched off his old television and sat down on a large brown leather chair.

"Where is the Gruesome Report, Mrs. Wart?"

A drawer in the desk opened and out came a small hand clutching some papers.

"Thank you, Mrs.Wart!" He took the papers and closed the drawer just as the hand disappeared back inside.

"Now as you are aware St. Squirmings has always done very well in the Gruesome Inspections. Up until this year!" He banged his fist on the desk. There was a groan from inside.

"You have let us down! Your thoughtfulness and kindness has brought St. Squirmings into disrepute!"

He stabbed his finger in the air.

"However, there is hope, we have been given five days to improve things. There is light at the end of the tunnel, children, we can only pray it is the light of an oncoming train! So it's down to you! I want something that will restore St.Squirmings' name. Something blood-curdlingly, stomach-turningly, nose-wipingly gruesome!"

He drummed his fingers on the table.

"And I want it by Friday!"

CHAPTER TWO

A crack of lightning lit up the school laboratory. It was late at night and all was quiet inside the classroom, but outside the thunder crashed and the rain poured. If anyone had dared to pass by the classroom of St. Squirmings so late at night they would have heard the creak of a window being opened, they would have heard the sound of four pairs of feet clambering onto the classroom floor and the sight they saw would have sent them screaming into the night.

Gordon, Franny, Benedict and Wilf stood in the centre of the dark room and looked about. Wilf shook his body like a dog and covered everyone with water.

"I hope I don't get a cold!" he said.

Benedict sniffed and wiped his neck hole with a hanky. He mumbled something.

"Yes, we know you already have a cold!" said Franny, "Now can we get to work?"

Gordon set about collecting scientific equipment. Test tubes, Bunsen burners, tubes and some chemicals. He wiped a tear from his eye as he did so.

"It reminds me of when I was first made!" He placed a hand on his creator's shoulder. She shrugged it off.

"If this is going to work – we need to concentrate!"

They all concentrated. Benedict sniffed.

"We need to make sure St. Squirmings gets good marks in its Gruesome Report. So this is my plan. I'm going to use all my scientific skills to create a new creature. We'll show it to Mr.Sneers and he'll be so impressed he'll show it to the Inspector and the Inspector will be so impressed he'll give us top marks!"

Wilf was looking at the equipment.

"But what are you going to make?"

Franny smiled deviously and Gordon giggled slightly behind his hand.

"I am going to create ... a Giant Worm!"

A clap of thunder smacked the air and Franny cackled manically.

Gordon strode over to a nearby tank and sunk his hand into the soil. He tugged out a long, thin, slimy worm. It wriggled.

Franny unfurled a large piece of paper and flattened it out on the table.

"Now if my plans are correct," said Franny, "And they usually are! All I need to do is place Chemical X3 into Chemical Z9. Put in the worm and puff - the worm will be a hundred times larger!"

Franny grasped a test tube full of bubbling Chemical X3 and poured it into a dish. It bubbled and frothed. She took a small bottle from her pocket.

"Z9!" she announced, showing the others.

"Z9?" hissed Wilf, "But that's Mrs. Stain's *special* chemical. Where did you get it?"

"I stole it from her at lunchtime!" Franny smiled and opened the bottle. She tipped a tiny amount into the dish. It fizzed and hissed, violently. A tiny drop plopped on the floor and sizzled on the varnish.

"Now insert the worm!"

The worm was winding itself around Gordon's thumb.

Suddenly, Gordon slipped on the chemical slippage. The worm jumped off his finger, shot through the air and disappeared into Benedict's neck-hole with a plop.

"Bother!" said Gordon.

"Achoooooooo!" said Benedict. The worm was suddenly shot out of Benedict's neck hole, flew through the air and splattered against the wall. It slid down onto a desk in a slimy heap.

"Oh, for goodness' sake!" said Franny. "Gordon, get up! Benedict wipe your neck! Wilf get another worm."

Benedict began tapping Franny on the shoulder.

"I think my knee's gone funny, mistress!" said Gordon. "Give me a tug!"

Benedict tapped Franny's shoulder again.

Franny grasped Gordon's hand and pulled him to his feet.

Benedict tapped her shoulder a final time.

"Stop tapping me, Benedict!" demanded Franny. Then she saw Gordon's face was frozen, staring at something behind her. She looked at Wilf who was also staring at something behind her.

Franny slowly turned.

There in the centre of the school laboratory was a big, green slimy monster. It had a long nose, drooping eyes and gaping mouth. It waved something Franny guessed was an arm.

"Hello!" said Franny. It waved another arm. It seemed to have quite a few.

"What is it?" hissed Wilf, out of the corner of his mouth.

"I don't know, but it's very green and slimy!" she replied.

"Wherever could it have come from?" asked Gordon.

Benedict sniffed and wiped his neck.

They all turned to look at Benedict.

Then they looked at the bubbling chemical dish.

Then they looked at the green, slimy creature.

"Benedict!" said Franny, very, very slowly. "Did you sneeze in the dish?"

Benedict didn't have a head, but it was clear from his movements he was slowly nodding.

"I can't believe it!" exclaimed Franny. "We've created a Snot Monster!"

Twenty minutes later the Snot Monster was sitting in the corner of the laboratory playing with the worm while the others discussed what to do.

"Can't you reverse the experiment?" asked Wilf.

"No, she can't!" said Gordon, quickly.

Whilst they were talking Benedict was writing. He scribbled away and then held up his piece of paper.

"Why don't we use the monster as the gruesome thing the Head wanted us to find?" it said.

Franny clicked her fingers.

"Of course, it's perfect! This is the answer – everyone will love us now! I have created the most gruesome thing imaginable!"

The monster looked a little hurt.

"No offence!" said Franny.

She gathered everyone around her.

"Right, we're going to show everyone at St. Squirmings we can be as gross as them. We are going to unveil our Snot Monster at assembly and we're going to do it first thing tomorrow morning!"

CHAPTER THREE

A large rusty cage stood in the great hall covered by a sheet.

Mr. Sneers sat on a high-backed chair tapping his foot. By his side sat Mrs. Grotter, cleaning her fangs with a hanky.

Franny coughed nervously and stood up. All the faces in the room turned to her and everyone fell silent.

"Good morning, everyone! As you know Mr. Sneers recently accused me and my friends of spoiling the schools Gruesome Report. Well, we are here today to prove we can be just as horrid as you!"

She surveyed the school and saw what a horrid lot it was. She took a deep breath and said,

"And so I have created a monster!"

A whoop of delight went up. Everyone knew about Gordon and they were very excited that Franny had created another.

"A filthy, vile and nasty monster!"

Another cheer and some clapping.

Zack the Zombie stood up. His face was half in light, half in shadow.

"It's a trick!" he heckled. "Don't believe her!"

The school children started muttering. Maybe it was a con, maybe she was trying to make them looked stupid.

"It's a typical goody-goody trick! Pretending to be bad, but not really meaning it!"

People started nodding their heads and agreeing with Zack.

Franny shouted above the muttering.

"I present – the Snot Monster!"

She tugged at the sheet and it fell to the ground.

Once more she surveyed the crowd. Now they'd love her, now they would want her to be nasty with them. Excellent! She had expected a small round of applause so she repeated :

"The Snot Monster!"

Zack laughed a hollow laugh and pointed at the cage.

"Snot there!"

Franny turned. The cage was empty! A slimy trail of snot led from the cage and out of the room. The Snot Monster had disappeared.

The entire school started to laugh and jeer and point at Franny. She stamped her foot.

Mr. Sneers stood up and plucked an eyebrow hair.

"Well, what a useless display that was. I'd like you all to join me and show her utter contempt!"

He blew a loud, spitty raspberry and the whole school joined in.

Franny ran from the room.

Outside in the school yard near the compost heap where Mr.Sneers kept his pets, Wilf, Gordon, Benedict and Franny were discussing the Snot Monster. They had worked out it had escaped from the cage by oozing itself through the bars. But where had it oozed to?

Benedict stood by a wheelie bin and gestured towards it madly. No one ever listens to me, he thought, I wish I still had my head then I would have something to say. He slapped the bin to get the attention of the others.

"We could catch the Monster in the wheelie bin!" announced Wilf.

Benedict shoved up two thumbs in delight.

"Very good idea, Master Wilf!" said Gordon, patting him on the back.

Benedict sighed, again.

The trail was followed and thirty minutes later the Snot Monster had been tracked down to the school canteen.

"AAArrrggghhhhh!!!"

Mrs. Singe was standing on a stool squealing like a scolded cat and pointing her ladle at the Monster as the four entered the room. The Snot Monster was gurgling with delight.

"Don't worry, Mrs. Singe, we'll take care of everything!"

"You'd better!" she trembled, "And don't get any of your fresh dirt on my food. You know I only use dirty dirt!"

Benedict placed the wheelie bin on its side outside the canteen door. He held up the lid and stood by it. Franny, Gordon and Wilf gathered some noisy cooking tools – spoons and bowls - and headed for the other entrance to the canteen.

As they did so Mr. Sneers walked past and noticed all the equipment in their arms.

"Are you three behaving yourselves?" he asked.

"Yes, sir!" said Wilf.

"Well, stop it at once!" he said and strode off.

The three entered the canteen from the far end and saw Mrs. Singe shivering on the stool. They could also see the slimy tip of the Snot Monster's head above the oven and they knew Benedict was on the other side of the door with the wheelie bin. All they had to do was chase the Snot Monster into it.

Franny whispered, "1...2...3..."

They suddenly started banging and clattering away on their tools. Crash, bang and a very loud wallop! The Snot Monster swivelled his head and saw all three heading towards him. He turned and bolted for the door, leaped through and crashed straight into the wheelie bin. Benedict slammed the lid shut, tilted it on to its wheels and then leaped on top. He dusted his hands and his shoulders shook with a giggle. The others soon joined him.

Word quickly got around the school that the monster had been captured and the corridors were lined with cheering ghouls and monsters. The wheelie bin was proudly wheeled along with Benedict sitting on top, waving. He'd even shredded a page of an exercise book which he threw in the air for extra effect. Franny, Wilf and Gordon joined in the applause.

From out of the crowd stepped Mr. Sneers. He eyed the foursome with suspicion.

"Are you four behaving yourselves?"

"Ye..." began Wilf, then he changed his mind, "No, sir, no we're not!"

And a huge cheer went up.

"Then come into my office!"

A few seconds later, with the Snot Monster safely parked outside, Franny, Wilf, Gordon and Benedict sat in Mr. Sneers' office. This was a special occasion and Mr. Sneers brought out some treats.

"Cup of cold slime, anyone?"

He poured out the drinks and then produced some moudly biscuits. Benedict rubbed the biscuit into crumbs and poured them into his neck hole follow by some cold slime. The Head found that pleasingly disgusting.

"Well, I must say I am impressed. Not long ago you were the worst pupils St. Squirmings had ever seen. Kind, courteous, thoughtful. It was awful. But I'm glad you've seen the error of your ways. And this Snot Monster sounds splendid and I think..!"

Franny interrupted.

"We should show it to the Gruesome Inspector!"

Mr. Sneers slurped his slime noisily and then wiped his lips on his sleeve.

"Hmm, well done for interrupting. That's exactly what I was going to say, "Wheel in the Snot Monster!"

Benedict skipped merrily out of the door.

"It is **very** disgusting?" asked Mr. Sneers.

"It might make you sick!" replied Wilf.

"Splendid!"

The door creaked open and the wheelie bin was wheeled in.

Mr. Sneers rose from his desk, rubbed his hands gleefully and threw open the lid. He gazed in.

Suddenly the Snot Monster leaped out, threw its many, slimy arms around Mr. Sneers and gave him a huge, slurping kiss. Then it jumped from the bin, oozed across the office and leaped into the sink. It poured itself down the plughole and giggled as it went. There was a loud, sticky burping sound and within seconds the giggling was nothing more than a distant echo.

Mr. Sneers wiped the snot from his lips.

The plants on the windowsill fluttered and slowly pointed their sharp leaves at the four pupils.

"Detention for the lot of you!" screeched Mr.Sneers.

CHAPTER FOUR

Franny wrote, "I must try harder to be naughty."

Wilf wrote, "Being nice is wrong."

Benedict wrote, "I'm bad for being good."

And Gordon wrote, "Until this moment, my behaviour had been considerate, cordial and congenial, so I herein promise to hereafter behave in a more thoughtless, unpleasant and anti-social manner." Then he winced when he realised he had to write it out one hundred times.

Mr. Sneers paced up and down in the classroom muttering under his breath and plucking his eyebrows.

"But, sir, we tried our best!" Franny suddenly snapped.

Mr. Sneers stopped.

"What did you call me?"

Franny sighed and tried again.

"But, fish face, we tried our best!"

"Best?"

"I mean worst."

Franny explained all about the giant worm she had planned and the how the Snot Monster appeared.

"Well, Franny, I'm afraid your worst wasn't bad enough. If there ever was a Snot Monster..." Mr. Sneers placed his face in front of Franny. She could smell his breath. Mouldy cheese and rotten eggs.

"Where is it now?"

And that was a question everyone was asking.

Far away on the other side of town in a dark, dark alley a shadowy figure was cackling to himself. The shadowy figure was dragging a large trunk from the back of a tatty old van.

The trunk hit a puddle with a splosh and from inside came a muffled groan.

The shadowy figure cackled some more as he scraped the trunk along the alleyway towards a door.

His weaselly little eyes darted back and forth to make sure no one was looking and he produced a small key, which he slid easily into the keyhole.

The door creaked open.

Inside the place had a strange smell. It was the smell of a hundred different animals. There was a screech, then a bark, then a whoop. The weaslley-eyed man dragged the trunk into the black room.

In the darkness he stumbled past crates and boxes muttering as he went. But he didn't notice the horrid smell. This was a smell he'd smelt a thousand times before.

He stopped in the centre of the room. The moon cast an eerie light across his face and his trunk.

He patted the trunk and a muffled moan came out.

"Don't worry, sweet one," he gestured towards the room, "This is your new home."

He started to unlock the lid, but then stopped.

The door was still open.

He scuttled over, poked his head out to check all was clear then slowly creaked the door shut.

The sign on the outside of the door read –

"Noah Zark, Pet Emporium."

He rested a moment then produced a crow bar and cracked open the lid.

He placed the crowbar to one side. He felt around inside and gently pulled out the occupant. It was a black bat. He shook it slightly.

"The sleeping drug will soon wear off, my sweet one!"

He carried the bat over to a mirror and wiped away a cobweb. He gazed at the reflection of them both.

"We both know you're a normal bat – but with a few changes here and there and perhaps a little paint I can make you look like a strange and exotic creature!" He grinned a toothless grin in the mirror, "Which some folk would pay a lot of money for!" He cackled once more. "But now, for a little refreshment!"

He walked over to the sink and held the drugged bat with one hand and while the other reached for the kettle.

At that point he heard giggling.
He looked about.

He heard it again then laughed to himself.

"Too many late nights," he said to the bat curled on his arm. "I'm starting to imagine things!"

Then there was a gurgling, some more giggling and a tremendous whooshing gush. Then a pop.

Noah Zark nearly dropped the bat.

There standing in the sink, up to its knees in dish water, was the Snot Monster.

It had travelled through the rusty pipes from St. Squirmings, somehow found its way to the pet shop and come up through the overflow pipe outlet.

Noah stared at the strange vision.

The Snot Monster waved and giggled.

Noah very slowly placed the bat back in the crate.

"Sleep well, sweet one," he said, sliding the lid on the crate. "But I've just had a much, much better idea!"

He turned to the Snot Monster.

"I don't know who you are or what you are, but you're going to make me a lot of money!"

The Snot Monster sloshed his way out of the sink, threw his arms around Noah and gave him a huge, sloppy kiss.

The next day Wilf and Franny were jogging to school. They'd never jogged before and were finding it hard work. They were in training. Gordon trailed behind in a kind of half-skip, half-wander.

Wilf punched the air a couple of times and tried some test questions.

"Okay, what's the best use for vegetable soup!"

Franny thought, then said, "Put it in a plastic bag and pretend you've been sick."

"Who would you give it to?"

"Ermm... the lollipop lady!"

"Excellent, see we can be gross. Me now."

Franny jogged on the spot whilst she thought.

"If a little old lady asks if you can see her across the road what do you do?" she asked.

"I know this one. I go across the road and say, 'Yep, I can see you!' then run off! High five!"

Franny slapped her hand in the air. Wilf slapped Franny around the face.

"Sucker!"

He ran on.

She ran after him and, breathlessly, Gordon followed. He eventually caught up with them.

"Could we ... slow...down...a... little!"

Wilf and Franny stopped by a shop.

"Stop?" asked Wilf, "That would be very..."

Franny joined in.

"Considerate!" They both cried and sped off. Gordon followed behind.

None of them took any notice of the shop they had stopped by. If they had they would have seen a very interesting sign in the window.

"Coming Soon – the Worlds Last Unicorn!"

It was a pet shop.

At the school gates Franny and Wilf skidded to a halt. Gordon nearly skidded into them. They gasped at what they saw.

Benedict, who always got to school first, was being jeered at by the other school kids. Zack the Zombie was pushing him back and forth. Various vampires were grabbing at his arms and shoving him back and forth. Wilf was about to jump in and save his friend, but Franny held him back.

"We can't be *good* anymore. Remember?" she said, sadly.

Suddenly from nowhere a louder chant started.

"On with his head! On with his head!"

And from behind the bike shed, Zack produced a carved pumpkin with a strange smile and a spluttering candle inside.

The others held Benedict tightly whilst Zack held the smiling head in the air.

"I place this head upon your shoulders! And crown you King of the Pumpkin Heads!" He lowered the head onto Benedict who had long since given up struggling. The school kids laughed and poked Benedict.

The shrill school bell rang and Mr.Sneers came to the front door.

"Get your smelly bodies into class!" he yelled, then burped loudly.

The school kids gathered all their books and jostled through the door almost toppling the Head.

"Well done, Hyde, good elbowing!"

Zack tried to push past, but Mr. Sneers stopped. He nodded towards Benedict who was slumped on the playground.

"Was that your idea, Zack?"

"What's it got to do with you, fish face?"

Mr. Sneers sighed.

"Just answer the question and stop trying to impress me."

Zack nodded.

"Yes, all my idea!"

"Very, very good work, Zack. You'll go far!"

Zack beamed broadly, sneezed on Mr. Sneers and ran off into class. Mr. Sneers followed him in, beaming proudly.

Wilf, Franny and Gordon crowded around the sad Benedict and helped him to his feet. They very gently removed his head.

Franny slowly said.

"It's no good! This lot will never respect us until..."

Wilf looked up at the moon and howled loudly.

"...We recapture the Snot Monster!"

CHAPTER FIVE

Mr. Sneers looked at the school through his good eye.

"Listen carefully! We're having a change of classes today. If you normally do Spot Squeezing with Mrs. Squelch, today you will be doing Dribbling for Beginners. If you're in the top class for Coughing then today you will be joining Year 3 for a film on Ear Wax. This is because Mrs. Squelch fell into a bath of cold custard this morning!"

The assembly sniggered.

"And I'm proud to introduce you to the pupil who pushed her!"

All heads turned as he announced.

"Zack Zombie!"

Zack swaggered forward with his arms in the air and a big smirk spread across his face.

Mr. Sneers held out his hand. Zack shook it and suddenly started shuddering uncontrollably. Mr. Sneers let go.

"It's an electric shocker. It's just my way of saying thank you!"

He suddenly bellowed, "Go to your classes!"

The pupils left the hall, shouting and screaming. Mr. Sneers turned to Zack.

"What class are you in this morning, Zack?"

Zack shrugged.

"I'm not doing any classes this morning, fish face! I'm having the day off!"

Mr. Sneers patted Zack on the shoulder.

"Oh, if we only had more like you!"

Zack walked down the street pleased to be missing school. Whenever he saw a stranger he'd put his arms in front of him and groaned, menacingly. This usually sent them off screaming.

The chip shop was open and Zack needed some cold chip fat for a school project so he nipped in. The shop owner eventually gave him some after he threatened to empty the contents of his pockets into the chip fryer. He helped himself to the cold fat and a big cone of chips and made off down the street.

He eventually arrived at his destination: Noah Zark – Pet Emporium

He opened the door.

"Dad!" yelled Zack, placing the bucket of chip fat on the counter. "You in?"

The weaslley-faced man scuttled from the back room.

"Shhhh! You'll wake the moles."

He opened a big book and started scribbling notes.

"Want a chip?" asked Zack, waving one under his nose.

"No, I don't! I'm working – and so should you be!"

Zack dipped his hand in a nearby fish tank and pulled out a flapping goldfish.

"Don't eat the pets!" snarled his father.

"But I always have fish with my chips!" Noah stared at his son and Zack dropped the fish back into the tank. It swam off quickly.

"Why aren't you at school?" spat Noah.

"Having the day off!"

The weaslley-faced man threw down his pen.

"However are you going to grow in to a proper zombie if you don't do your lessons?" he sighed.

Zack decided to change the subject.

"How's the new arrival?"

Zack's father looked about.

"It's well, very well. Not sure what to feed it, but I'll soon sell it so that won't matter."

Zack drew closer to his father.

"What you going to sell it as?"

Father cackled and dribbled slightly with delight.

"The World's Last Unicorn!"

Zack chewed his last chip.

"That's brilliant, Dad, really brilliant. You got any buyers yet?"

Father sighed.

"Not yet. I still need to add the finishing touches."

Zack was about to scrunch up his cone and hurl it in with the snakes, when his father stopped him. He snatched the cone from his hand and held it up.

"Brilliant, son, brilliant, that's just what I need!"

Wilf, Benedict, Gordon and Franny came running out of the pizza shop. Right behind them came the owner clutching in his hand a large pizza.

"You idiots! Look what you've done to my pizza!"

They stopped and turned.

"I said, 'Shall I season it?'" he yelled.

Wilf shouted, "We thought you said, 'Can you sneeze on it?' - so we did!"

The group high-fived and ran off.

Further down the street they stopped breathless by a shop.

"Excellent!" said Franny. "See we can be gross if we really try!"

Benedict's attention was caught by something else.

"Indeed, that was quite a foul thing to do, mistress!" agreed Gordon, patting his nose with a hanky.

Benedict was tapping the window of the shop.

"So what are we going to do next?" asked Wilf, "Something really foul..."

Benedict was tapping the window louder and louder. They all turned to see what he was pointing at. They gasped when they saw what it was.

"The Snot Monster!"

It sat in the corner looking sad and sniffing slightly.

Franny peered closer.

"It's a got a polystyrene cone tied to its head!" she exclaimed.

Wilf pointed at the sign.

"The World's Last Unicorn!" he read. "But it's our Snot Monster! We've got to get it back!"

At that point Zack the Zombie came out of the shop.

"You!" shouted Franny, "You stole our monster!"

"So?" shrugged Zack and flicked her nose, "It's my dad's Snot Monster now and..." he gurgled with delight, "He's selling it!"

Benedict pushed past Zack into the shop.

"That is such a low thing to do!" said Wilf.

"Thank you very much!" replied Zack, proudly and skipped off down the road.

The others followed Benedict inside.

Zack's father was looking a little bewildered at the headless monk who was banging the counter and pointing at the window.

"Alright, alright, don't lose your head! What do you want? Do you want to buy a mole?"

Benedict shook his shoulders as the others joined him.

"Perhaps you might be interested in a slug? They're very friendly are slugs..."

Gordon pressed his face against the pet shop owners face and spoke very slowly.

"We want our monster back."

Zack's father tried to look as innocent as he could. He didn't find it easy.

"Oh, you mean the unicorn? That's the last one in the world, y'know. Not cheap."

Franny joined Gordon.

"That is OUR Snot Monster and we want it back!"

The pet shop owner looked at the faces of the pupils.

"You're obviously very keen to get your hands on my unicorn."

He wandered behind the counter.

"And if you're that keen – you'll be prepared to pay!"

Benedict started banging the counter again.

"But it's OURS!" cried Wilf.

Franny placed a hand over Benedict's fists and hushed Wilf.

"How much?" she said, quietly.

A smile wound itself around the pet shop owner's face.

"Well, it's very rare and you're, obviously, keen to have it – so I think I can ask a special price."

Franny took a deep breath.

"How much?"

"£3,000!"

Wilf and Franny sat on park bench eating soil sandwiches and Gordon and Benedict were sharing a Cornish Nasty.

"How are we going to get £3,000?" sighed Wilf.

A shadow fell across their faces and they all stopped and looked up. Before them was a tall lady with a caring and pleasant face. She was holding a tin.

"Good afternoon, I'm sorry to disturb you but I'm collecting for the local dogs' home. Would you like to put a little something in my tin?"

Wilf started searching his pockets for a little something.

Franny stopped him before he could frighten the lady.

"How much money do you collect?"

The lady thought for a moment then said, "Some days a few pounds, but some days we can raise hundreds and hundreds!"

Franny produced a pound coin and dropped it in the tin.

"Thank you!" said the lady and moved on.

"I thought we were being naughty, mistress?" Gordon reminded her.

"We are, but that lady has just given me a brilliant idea!"

CHAPTER SIX

The doorbell at Mrs. Nightingale's cottage rang brightly. She put down her cup of tea and made her way down the hall. She opened the door. Before her stood three choir singers. One short and female, one short, hairy and male, and the other tall with a large head and green skin. They began to sing.

"Good King Wenceslas looked out on the feast of Stephen."

Mrs. Nightingale held up a hand.

The singers stopped.

"It's the 12th of July!" she said, sharply.

Franny shifted uncomfortably. It was all her idea, anyway and the others hadn't been convinced it was a good one.

55

Behind the hedge Benedict sniggered. Franny had banned him from being part of the choir in case he frightened people.

"But we're collecting for a good cause!" responded Franny, "Remember we met you earlier. We gave you a pound coin!"

"What *good cause*?" asked Mrs. Nightingale.

Wilf rattled a can, "We're collecting money to save the world's last unicorn!"

Mrs. Nightingale was suddenly very thrilled.

"The world's last unicorn! That's very kind and considerate of you!"

Franny looked about to make sure no one from school heard her praise.

"Yes, well, keep it to yourself, will you?"

Mrs. Nightingale produced a small purse, removed a coin and slipped it into Wilf's can.

"Congratulations – it is so rewarding to see children being responsible and charitable. Do you know 'Away in a Manger'?"

"No!" said Franny and they ran off down the drive.

Mrs. Nightingale closed the door of the cottage. She was so thrilled by the pupils' act of generosity that she decided more people should know about it.

She picked up the telephone in the hall.

"Hello, is that Sunshine Television?"

Franny had had the idea of dressing like choristers and going from house to house singing carols and raising money. She thought it was a good idea. The others didn't. Gordon could hardly fit into the costume for a start and Benedict was annoyed he couldn't join in. Wilf, however, had a more practical attitude. He was convinced they'd never collect £3,000 by singing carols. And the contents of the tin proved he was right.

"£4.57 and a rubber band!" Gordon finally announced after a recount. They were sitting on a wall near the swings.

"This is ridiculous – I said we'll never raise £3,000 this way!"

Suddenly from out of her cottage appeared Mrs. Nightingale.

"There they are!" she shrieked and a man they had never seen before started running down the street towards them.

"She's called the police!" yelled Wilf, gathering the coins and starting to run off. Gordon grabbed Benedict and followed after. Franny, however, stayed exactly where she was.

The man was soon by her side. He was tall and handsome and looked like he had spent just a little too long under the sun tan machine.

Mrs. Nightingale spoke.

"Here she is! This is the little girl whose idea it was!"

"I'm Johnny Jason from Sunshine News," he smiled, "You might have heard of me."

Franny had heard of him, of course, he was the most famous face on local television.

"Doesn't ring a bell," she said, staring at her nails.

Further down the street the others stopped and turned.

"Well, Mrs. Nightingale tells me you've been doing some charity work. Could we interview you?"

The others slowly started to return.

Johnny Jason produced a microphone from his pocket and beckoned to a camerawoman who had been lurking behind a hedge.

"They're collecting to save the world's last unicorn!" declared Mrs.Nightingale, smartening herself to be interviewed. Johnny Jason ignored her.

"I hear you're collecting to save the world's last unicorn."

"Yes, that's correct, but I don't want to talk about it. I'm very modest." said Franny.

The camerawoman was zooming in on her and Johnny was thinking of another question.

"Well, it's such a good cause. Maybe Sunshine Television could make a contribution?"

Gordon and Benedict were at Franny's side.

"What do your friends think?"

Gordon was nodding eagerly. So was Benedict, though it was difficult to tell.

"How much would be a fair contribution?"

Wilf joined them.

"How about £2,995.43?"

Johnny Jason nearly dropped his microphone.

He mumbled something to his camerawoman and then pulled out a mobile phone. He punched in a number and mumbled into it. He finished the call then turned to Franny. He was smiling.

"£2,995.43, it is!"

Wilf leaped up and howled with delight. He suddenly stopped and said, "How about an extra £5,000 as well?"

Franny grabbed him by the collar and marched him away from the rest of the group.

"He's agreed to £2,995.43! That's all we need! We're going to get the money for the Snot Monster *and* win back our Gruesome Report!"

Wilf muttered an apology and they returned to the group. Johnny Jason began tidying himself and started talking to the camera.

Suddenly, Gordon shrieked.

"What if they recognise us?"

"Who?" asked Franny and Wilf.

"The rest of the school — they don't know we're buying back the Snot Monster.

They'll think we're doing a good deed and..." he sniffed, "...they'll hate us!"

Benedict thought quickly and rapidly ran to the nearest greengrocers. He returned just in time for the live interview.

It was with surprise Johnny Jason began interviewing four choristers each with a paper bag on their heads.

At the end of the interview Franny collected their money. She insisted on cash and they left giggling with delight and glee. "Good job no one recognised us!" shouted Wilf.

On the other side of town the Mr. Sneers was furiously plucking hairs from his eyebrows. He stabbed a finger into his remote control and his TV picture fizzle away.

"I'd recognise those voices anywhere! Collecting for charity? Collecting for charity?" He could hardly say the words, "I've obviously been too lenient with these pupils. It's about time they had some serious punishment.

He picked up the telephone.

"Mrs. Wart – prepare the rack!"

CHAPTER SEVEN

The large medieval rack stood in the centre of the Head Teacher's office. Franny, Gordon, Wilf and Benedict stood silently staring at the floor. The rack had shackles for hands and feet and the hands and feet in them belonged to Mr. Sneers.

"Turn the handle two more notches, Franny!" he instructed.

Franny did so and Mr. Sneers bones cracked loudly.

"Ah, that's better! I like a nice stretch!"

Mrs. Wart's hand was reaching out of the desk drawer stirring Mr. Sneers' tea.

"Bring me my tea, Wilf!"

Wilf did as he was instructed. Mr. Sneers continued his telling off.

"St.Squirmings has only one day left to improve its Gruesome Report. And you four go and appear on television as charity collecting choristers!"

Wilf poured a few drops of tea into Mr. Sneers' mouth. He slurped loudly. He stopped. He stared up at the mug Wilf was holding and suddenly spat out the contents.

"Miss Wart! I always have three salts in my tea!"

Wilf returned the mug to the desk, slopping the remaining contents on some papers.

The hand emerged with a teaspoon and put two more salts into the mug.

"Better!" snarled the Head and craned his head to the pupils.

The hand made a rude gesture and slammed the drawer shut as it went.

"Explain!" he snapped.

"We were trying to find something really gross so the Inspector would be really repulsed..." began Franny.

"And you thought singing 'Silent Night' dressed as choristers would do the trick, did you?"

Gordon spoke.

"If I could interject momentarily."

"Why does he talk like that?" asked Mr. Sneers, suspecting Gordon might be a little more educated than himself.

"Miss Franny is quite correct in her assertion. Initially we were to create a giant worm!"

Mr. Sneers arched his eyebrows in surprise. A giant worm would certainly have gained them some points.

"But, sadly, Benedict sneezed on the chemical dish and we merely created a monster made of snot."

Mr. Sneers tried to drum his fingers on the rack.

"Back to the old snot story, eh?"

The pupils nodded.

"Detention for the lot of you!"

Franny stamped her foot.

"That is the most unfair, disgusting and vile thing I've ever heard."

Mr. Sneers snorted, noisily.

"You won't get round me that way!" he said as they stomped out the room.

"That's taught them a lesson." He cackled gleefully, "You can untie me now, Mrs. Wart!"

There was no reply.

"Mrs. Wart?"

The plants on the window sill fluttered and closed up

"Mrs. Wart............?"

Mrs. Scratcher was in charge of detention. Luckily for the pupils she was a little bit dreamy and spent the session engrossed in a book about Dracula.

"He's just so hunky!" she said as a knock came to the door, "Come in if you want to bite my neck!"

Zack the Zombie entered with a large sack.

"No, thanks! Mr. Sneers says I've got to take the worms!"

At the back of the class was a large glass tank containing earth worms.

"Help yourself!" she said and plunged back into her novel.

Zack sneered at Franny as he walked past dragging his sack.

"Goodie-goodies got detention!" he chanted, "I'm getting worms for my dad! We're going to sell them as Peruvian water snakes! They're really popular at the moment!"

Franny could hardly contain her indignation. Her hand shot up in the air.

Mrs. Scratcher sighed and placed a bookmark in her novel.

"Yes, little girl, what is it?"

"Zack just lied to you!"

Wilf and Gordon nodded in agreement.

"Did he indeed?"

"Yes!" they chorused.

"Well, that's a point for your team, Zack!"

Zack stuck up a thumb and then turned his attention to the worms.

A few minutes later the bell shattered the silence.

Mrs. Scratcher slapped her book closed.

"Detention over! Franny?"

"Yes,miss!" She handed in her work.

"Get lost! Wilf?"

"Yes,miss!" He handed in his work.

"Get lost! Gordon?"

"I think the textbook was incorrect in the section on..."

"Get lost! Benedict?"

There was no reply, but no one was surprised as Benedict didn't have a mouth. But on this occasion he didn't have a body, either.

"Benedict? Ah, well! Get lost all of you!"

She scuttled out of the door.

But where was Benedict?

The bell tinkled as Zack entered the Pet Shop dragging his sack behind him. His father slithered into the room.

"What you got me?" he hissed.

"Peruvian Water Snakes!"

His father looked down at the sack and spat.

"I can't afford Peruvian Water Snakes!"

"I know, that's why I got a bag of earth worms. You just have to tell the punters they're Water Snakes. We should get a tenner each for 'em!"

He punched his son playfully, pulled a large knife from behind the counter and sliced off the top of the sack.

He peered in.

Suddenly the doorbell tinkled again and in walked a small man holding a magnifying glass. He wore his hat very, very low down.

The man slapped some cash on the counter. £3,000 to be exact.

Noah looked about suspiciously. He pushed the sack of worms to one side and gestured to Zack to pull down the blinds.

The man pointed at the money, mumbled something and pointed to the window.

"You want to buy a mole?"

The man shook his hat.

"Very cheap the mole…" He looked at the money on the counter, "I can get you 3,000 moles for that money!"

The man banged the counter and pointed towards the window once more.

Noah leaned closer to the man.

"I'm sorry, sir, I can't understand a word you're saying. Perhaps if I removed your hat!"

Noah reached across and removed the hat. Underneath the hat there was no head.

Noah blinked.

He looked inside the hat.

There was no head in the hat, either.

Then he screamed.

"Aaarrrrghhh!! His head's come off! His head's come off in my shop!"

He started to skip on the spot. He pointed at Zack and then at the headless man.

"No head!" he screamed.

Zack placed a comforting arm on his father's shoulder.

"That's because he's Benedict, the headless monk! We go to school together!"

Zack soon calmed his father down and explained all about Benedict. But what did he want?

"What do you want?" asked Noah, still trembling slightly.

It wasn't long before Benedict had made it clear to Zack and his father what he wanted. Mainly by banging his fist against the shop window and pointing at the Snot Monster.

"Oh, the Unicorn!" Noah finally understood, "That's £3,000!"

Benedict handed over the notes and Zack slowly opened the cage as his father counted them.

"That's correct! £3,000 exactly! The world's last unicorn is yours. Would you like it gift wrapped?"

But Benedict and the Snot Monster didn't hear the question. They were already out on the street with the shop's bell left tinkling behind them.

There were some strange looks as a headless monk and a large monster made of snot took the No. 27 bus down the High Street.

CHAPTER EIGHT

The grey clouds spat down cold rain on the hearse as it slowly made its way up the driveway of St. Squirmings.

The school was well-prepared for the return visit of the Inspector and everything had been done to make the school look as uninviting as possible. Books had been burned, many of the toilets had been pulled out and smashed and a lot of the wallpaper had been torn off. They were determined to achieve the top marks this time.

As the hearse drew up in front of the school doors someone sneezed on it. Mr. Poke was tugged out of his coffin by two hairy prefects, who burped loudly and then sent him off in the wrong direction three different times. The Inspector thought that was very impressive.

Finally, he found his way to the Mr. Sneers office.

"Get lost!" he said in the traditional greeting.

"Stick it in your ear!" replied Mr. Sneers in the timeworn manner, "Mrs. Wart – make our guest welcome!" A hand emerged from the desk and made a rude gesture she reserved for special occasions.

"I must say you're getting much better," said Mr. Poke, removing a mousetrap from a chair then sitting down. "You've almost got enough points to pass the inspection. I was very impressed with the toilets! "

"Yes," said Mr. Sneers, proudly, "They haven't been cleaned since 1927!"

"And the Staff Tomb is one of the untidiest I've ever seen!"

"I know!" said Mr.Sneers, "Could I offer you a mug of slime?"

"Goodness – that really is disgusting!" He made a big tick on his clipboard.

A knock came to the door.

"Get lost!" shouted the Head Teacher.

Mr. Poke nodded, impressed.

Franny's head appeared around the door.

"Excuse me, sir..."

Mr. Sneers coughed loudly and strode over to the door. He pushed Franny through it and into the corridor.

"Do you have to be so polite in front of the Inspector? Our Gruesome marks rely on this visit." He returned to the office and, smiling greasily, closed the door behind him.

The door flew open and crashed against the filing cabinet. There stood Franny with her arms folded.

"Oi, fish face!"

"Franny Stein, one of our more promising pupils," said Mr. Sneers, "She created a monster from human body parts, you know."

The Inspector was certainly impressed by the changes.

"Yes, I think I can safely say...." he began.

"Oi, I was talking!"

The Inspector almost giggled with delight.

"One really doesn't see that standard of interruption in many schools these days!"

Franny walked into the room.

"The Snot Monster's back, fish face, and it's in the hall!"

The Head shifted uncomfortably. He was convinced this was all make-believe. He decided to humour her.

"Very well, we'll be along shortly!"

Franny sniffed loudly, coughed and left.

"Delightfully horrid!" said the Inspector.

"Shall we go and see Year 3 – they're doing a project on dandruff!"

Mr. Poke stood up.

"No!" he said, "I want to see the Snot Monster!"

Benedict was running around the hall like a headless chicken. He had something to say, but couldn't say it. He kept stamping his foot and Gordon and Wilf were trying to understand him, The hall doors suddenly clanked open and in walked Mr.Sneers followed by Mr.Poke.

"Get stuffed!" shouted Wilf and Gordon.

"And the same to you!" replied the Head.

In the centre of the room was a large cage once more draped in a grotty sheet.

Franny entered, panting.

"It's no good I can't find...." She stopped when she saw the Head and the Inspector.

"Can't find what?" inquired Mr. Poke.

Franny thought quickly.

"What's it got to do with you, fish face?"

The Inspector turned to the Head.

"She really is *very* good, isn't she?"

Mr. Sneers was little nervous. He'd seen no evidence of a Snot Monster and didn't believe it existed. He was hoping he wasn't going to be made a fool of.

They drew up two chairs and sat down.

"Show us then, Franny!" he ordered.

Franny shifted from one foot to the other as if she wanted to go to the toilet.

"Well..." she began.

"Well?" replied Mr. Poke, getting comfy.

Gordon and Wilf were grasping the edges of the sheet ready to reveal the creature.

"The thing is..." continued Franny.

Benedict was trying to stop Wilf pulling off the sheet.

Mr. Poke looked at his watch.

"Do hurry I've got Year 4 Gargling in ten minutes!"

"Well, how can I put this..." Franny continued.

Gordon managed to wrestle Benedict from Wilf and with one hefty tug they pulled the sheet off the cage.

Mr. Poke gazed at the cage.

It was empty.

"We lost it!" explained Franny.

Mr. Sneers looked at the Inspector and tried to smile.

Mr. Poke leaped to his feet.

"Utter rubbish! I had high hopes for you my girl, but this is just utter rubbish." He made a cross on his clipboard then turned to Mr. Sneers.

"I really don't think I need to see anymore – you have failed your Gruesome!" he said and stomped from the hall.

Mr. Sneers glared at the four.

Benedict was still jumping up and down trying to explain.

The Head started to speak, but he was lost for words so made a rude noise and followed the Inspector.

Wilf broke the silence.

"So where is it now?"

Benedict pointed upwards.

They all looked to the ceiling.

"On the roof?" said Gordon.

Mr. Poke opened the hearse door and was climbing into his coffin as the Head scurried down the drive towards him.

"Inspector, please, I'm sure a minor hiccup, like this, won't spoil your report!"

Mr. Sneers pulled Mr. Poke out of the hearse, slammed the door shut and leaned against it.

"This is my life, Inspector, I've been here nearly three hundred years. I adore teaching children bad habits. My heart is in this school - and quite a few other organs, too! Your report could close us down."

"So?" said Mr. Poke, slowly.

"We're doing wonderful work here. We're raising money through bribery and corruption to build a new slime pool, Mrs. Scratcher has been asked to haunt a posh hotel! Please don't close us down!"

Mr. Poke drew his face close to Mr. Sneers. The Head could see the silhouette of his beloved St. Squirmings behind the Inspector.

"You are an idiot!" snapped Mr. Poke, "This is the worst Ghoul School in the country!"

The Head was crushed. That was the cruellest thing anyone had ever said to him. He looked past the Inspector to St. Squirmings. The rot on the walls, the broken windows, the rat infested staff room. How could he live without it? He looked up at the sagging roof - and then his expression changed.

High above the driveway, hanging onto a broken guttering was the Snot Monster. It was giggling.

Mr. Sneers blinked. He blinked again and then his face broke into something quite close to a smile.

"So get out of the way!" said the Inspector.

Benedict suddenly appeared next to the Monster on the roof and offered him his hand, but being headless couldn't quite make out where the monster was.

The Monster was chuckling and clinging to the pipe. Benedict stepped forward, the guttering snapped loudly. The Monster squealed and began to fall through the air. Mr. Poke turned and saw the monster plummeting towards him. With one huge gurgling squelch the monster splattered all over the Inspector.

For a moment there was a silence.
It was very long silence.

In the distance the raven squawked.

Gordon, Franny and Wilf came running into the driveway and quickly stopped when they saw the mess. There was a squelch and Mr. Poke slowly emerged out of the mess. He was covered from head to toe in snot.

The Snot Monster was splattered everywhere.

Mr. Sneers helped up the Inspector and became covered in snotty handmarks.

"How can I ever apologise?" he began. He pointed to his pupils, "Those stupid, stupid children. I tried to bring them up to be thoughtless and rude. How could they let me down?"

Then the Inspector started to giggle.

Then he started to laugh.

Then he started to guffaw.

They all gazed at him.

He wiped some slime from his face and said, "That is the most vile, gross and stomach-turningly gruesome thing that has ever happened to me..." He looked to the pupils, they waited for his next words, the Head plucked his eyebrows anxiously, "And I loved it!"

He threw his clipboard in the air and did a little dance.

"I've waited years for a school to do something as grotty as that! I'm so proud of you!"

He gave Mr. Sneers a big hug.

"You passed your Gruesome Inspection with flying colours!"

He picked up his clipboard.

"They will be so jealous of me back at the office!"

And with that he jumped into the hearse, slammed down the lid of his coffin and was driven away.

Franny looked at Wilf who looked at Gordon. They stood waiting for Mr.Sneers response as Benedict arrived. The faces of all the other pupils of the Ghoul School peered out of broken windows, pot holes and doorways. They nervously waited for his words.

"Have the rest of the day off!"

There was a huge cheer.

"Have the rest of the week off!"

There was an ever bigger cheer.

"Have the rest of the term off!"

There was the biggest cheer of all

"And if you want to thank anyone — thank these four." He pointed to Franny, Wilf, Gordon and Benedict, "The best worst pupils I've ever had the pleasure to teach!"

The cheering continued as the Head returned to the school.

The four star pupils stood alone on the driveway surrounded by the snotty remains of the monster.

"Poor Snot Monster!" said Franny, "I'm going to miss him." She pulled a handkerchief from her jacket and began wiping him up. Benedict found a mop and started mopping away the remains of the Snot Monster. He squeezed the slimy snot into a bucket.

Gordon appeared with a flask of slime and poured out four beakers.

"To the Snot Monster – keep your nose clean!"

And they all drank a large mouthful.

Then they turned and made their way back to St. Squirmings, once again the best Ghoul School in the country.

And on the bent and broken school gates the black raven squawked as the cold, cold rain slashed down all around

GET YOUR FREE BOOK

VISIT HERE - http://eepurl.com/bt9RLP

Poems! Stories! Jokes! Limericks! And Cheese!*
Enter the kooky world of International Kid's Comic and Writer IAN BILLINGS as he rummages in his lost property box to bring you a bonkers book of stuff!
His silly style and wacky words will take you on a giggle-filled, chuckle-stuffed gallop through his mad mind!
There's chickens and fish and doors and octopuses and honey and tyres and noses and monsters and eggs and insects and pirates and holes and owls and geckos and clippings and mermaids and butter and spam and hiccups and cheese.**
If you like laughing, you'll like IAN BILLINGS' LOST PROPERTY!
* There's no cheese in it....
** There really isn't any cheese....